The BAD
good manners
Book

The BAD good manners Book

Babette   Cole

Hamish Hamilton

Don't leave the taps on in the bathroom.

Don't fill the sink up
with hairs.

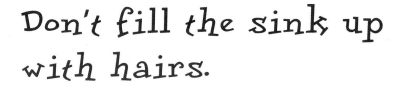

Don't bung the loo up
with paper.

Don't leave
your toys

on the stairs!

Don't mess around in the kitchen.

Don't dress up the dog . . .

or the cat!

Don't have a shampoo

with a big tube of glue,

and don't tell your mum

that
she's fat.

Do try

to dress
yourself

properly.

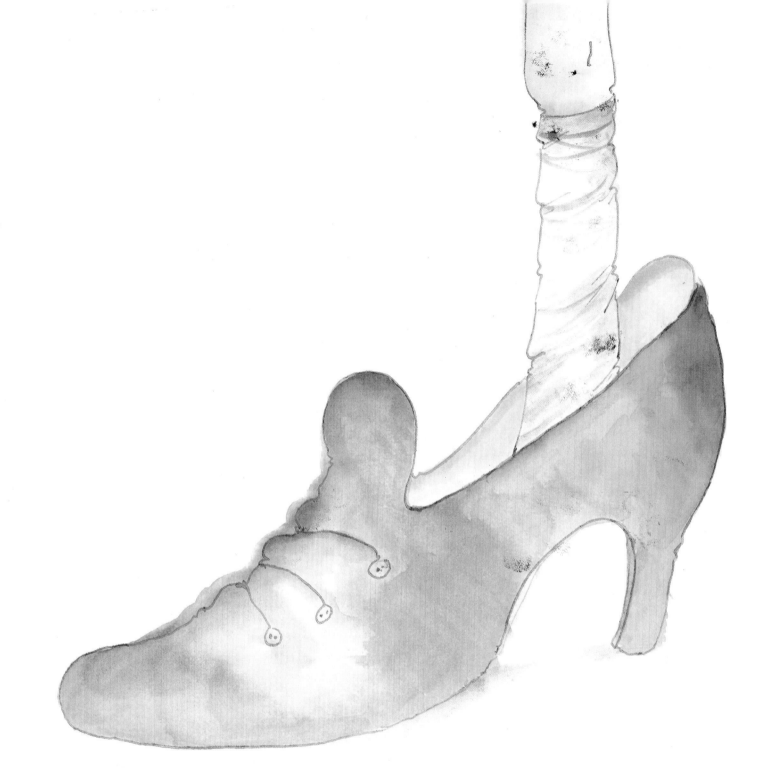

Do put the right shoes

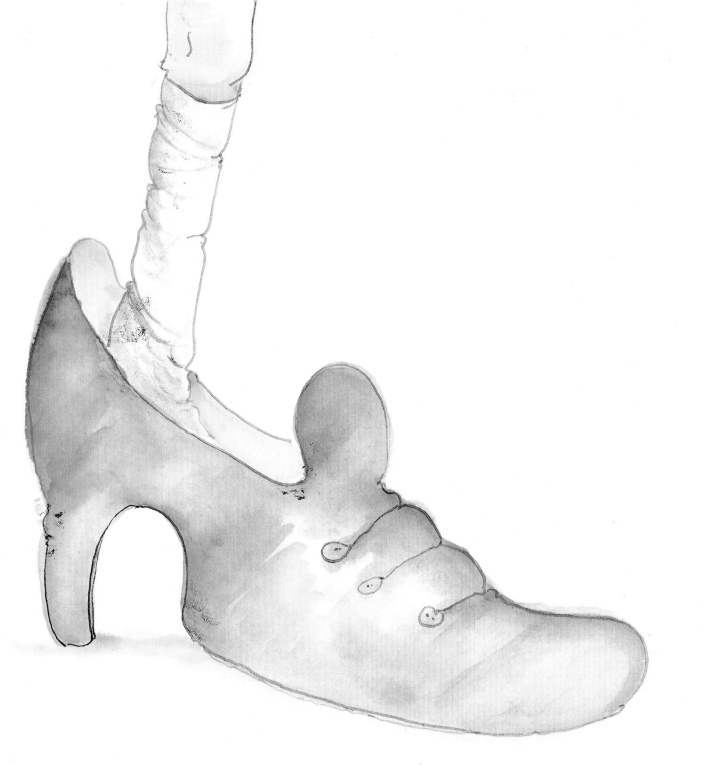

on your feet!

Do try to mind your own business . . .

it's very
unpleasant
to peep!

Do tidy your terrible bedroom.

Brush your hair,

clean
your teeth,

wash your hands!

Do as you would
be done by . . .

As much as you
possibly can!

"I was trying!"

HAMISH HAMILTON LTD

Published by the Penguin Group
27 Wrights Lane, London W8 5TZ, England
Penguin Books USA Inc, 375 Hudson Street, New York, New York 10014, USA
Penguin Books Australia Ltd, Ringwood, Victoria, Australia
Penguin Books Canada Ltd, 10 Alcorn Avenue, Toronto, Ontario, Canada, M4V 3B2
Penguin Books (NZ) Ltd, 182-190 Wairau Road, Auckland 10, New Zealand

Penguin Books Ltd, Registered Offices: Harmondsworth, Middlesex, England

First published in Great Britain 1995 by Hamish Hamilton Ltd

Text and illustrations copyright © 1995 by Babette Cole

1 3 5 7 9 10 8 6 4 2

The moral right of the author has been asserted

British Library Cataloguing in Publication Data
CIP data for this book is available from the British Library

ISBN 0-241-13478-1

Printed in Italy by L.E.G.O.